Catch a Gran

by

Diana Hendry

Illustrated by Kirstin Holbrow

You do not need to read this page –
just get on with the book!

First published in 2006 in Great Britain by
Barrington Stoke Ltd
www.barringtonstoke.co.uk

ISBN-10: 1-842993-71-2
ISBN-13: 978-1-84299-371-2

Printed in Great Britain by Bell & Bain Ltd

Meet The Author – Diana Hendry

What is your favourite animal?
Dog
What is your favourite boy's name?
Hamish, my son's name
What is your favourite girl's name?
Kate, my daughter's name

What is your favourite food?
Chips!
What is your favourite music?
Mozart
What is your favourite hobby?
Playing the piano

Meet The Illustrator – Kirstin Holbrow

What is your favourite animal?
My dog, Pewter Plum
What is your favourite boy's name?
George
What is your favourite girl's name?
Violet

What is your favourite food?
Sprouts
What is your favourite music?
Pop
What is your favourite hobby?
Rowing on the River Wye

To Paul,
with love,
Kirsti

Contents

Chapter 1
Wellies and One-eyed Ted

"Some holiday!" I said when Mum told me. Of course I was very sorry that Auntie Jean – she's Mum's sister – was ill and Mum had to go and look after her. But I was even more sorry that I had to go and stay with Grandad.

"It's the summer," I said, "and you're sending me off to the middle of nowhere." *The middle of nowhere* was how Mum and

Dad always talked about the place where Grandad lived.

"Forget the middle of nowhere," Dad said. "Where Grandad lives is more like the back of beyond." Then Dad laughed and said, "Joke! Joke!" because he'd seen my face.

"Not funny!" I said.

"Grandad lives in the country. In a cottage," said Mum.

"And he likes to live on his own," I said.

"That's only since your grandma died," said Dad. "Maybe you can cheer him up."

"It'll be me who needs cheering up," I said. "Grandad must be at least 200 years old."

"80," said Dad. "Grandad's only 80."

"Only!" I said.

"And it's just for a week, Molly," said Mum. "It'll be very interesting for you. A change from living in a town."

When Mum says something's going to be *very interesting*, you know what she means is very boring. My mum is a total town person. Shops. Cinemas. Cafés. That's what my mum likes. And so do I.

"The country," I said. "Cows and muddy fields and nothing happening. Why can't Dad look after me?"

"I have to go to work," said Dad. "I don't think Grandad has any cows. But you'd better take your wellies for the muddy fields."

"I could go and stay with Emma," I said. Emma's my best friend.

"They're going away on holiday," said Mum.

"Auntie Carol," I said. Auntie Carol is my dad's sister. She's very bossy and I don't like her much but I thought anything – *anyone* – would be better than Grandad.

"She's got visitors," said Mum, "so she won't have any room for you. We're going to put you on the train after school tomorrow."

Well, that was one thing to be glad about. I didn't want to miss the last day of term.

"We've arranged for the guard on the train to look after you," Mum told me. "Grandad will meet you at the station. And you'll need this," she said. From the cupboard she pulled out my red bike helmet.

4

"What's this for?" I asked.

"It's to protect you from pigs falling out of the sky!" said Dad. "Joke! Joke!"

"Your jokes are very unfunny," I said.

"Grandad has a tandem," said Mum.

"A what ...?"

"A tandem," said Dad. "It's a bicycle for two. Grandad and Grandma used to ride all over the place on the tandem. He'll collect you from the station on it."

"No car?" I asked.

"No car," said Mum. "But you're really good on your bike."

This is true, even if I say it myself. Last term I passed my cycling test. "Riding *my* bike is a bit different from riding a tandem – with a doddery old man," I said.

"I think you'll be surprised," said Dad. "I don't think Grandad's at all doddery. He's fit and strong."

"And anyway," said Mum, "he's doing us a big favour by looking after you for the week. So you be good and helpful."

"And try and have a good time!" said Dad.

I didn't answer that. I went off to my bedroom. I packed my oldest clothes, my wellies and lots of books and CDs. The bag got very heavy. I thought about Grandad's tandem and took out half of my stuff.

Then I went to bed. What Mum had said – *the middle of nowhere*, and Dad's joke – *the back of beyond*, went round and round in my head. I thought maybe the middle of nowhere was a muddy field that went on and on forever. As for the back of beyond, I thought that was some place at the end of the world.

I snuggled down in bed then. One-eyed Ted was waiting for me. "This is going to be the worst week of my life," I told him. "And you're coming too."

Chapter 2
A Slightly Smelly Grandad

"Think of it as an adventure," said Mum when she put me on the train.

The train *did* feel like an adventure. It was the first time Mum and Dad had let me travel on my own. I had a seat by the window. Mum gave me some sandwiches, two apples, one banana, two fruit bars and a bottle of water. Dad gave me a new puzzle book.

"You don't need to worry about when to get off the train," said Mum. "The guard will come and tell you."

There was a lady sitting in the seat across from me. "I'll keep an eye on your little girl," she told Mum.

I waved and waved and waved when the train started. Mum and Dad were standing on the platform and as the train left, they got smaller and smaller. And then I thought I might cry but I didn't want the lady who was keeping an eye on me to see. So I just sniffed a bit and blew my nose. I think the lady knew I was upset because she asked me if I wanted a biscuit and where I was going.

"I'm going to the middle of nowhere," I said. The lady laughed at that.

"Does the middle of nowhere have a name?" she asked.

"Yes," I said. "It's called Hamden. It's where my Grandad lives. I'm going to stay with him for a week."

"Well, you're very lucky," she said. "I've heard it's a very pretty place."

"I don't feel very lucky," I said. "My grandad's very, very old and I'm going to miss my friends."

"Maybe you'll meet new ones," said the lady.

"Like cows," I said. And the lady laughed again.

After that I did two puzzles from my new book, ate all the sandwiches and fell asleep. When I woke up it was getting dark and it was really nice and cosy on the train. I liked the sound of the train thrumming like the deep notes of a guitar. I

liked looking out of the window too. Sometimes we passed a village and saw houses lit up and street lights like big lanterns held up in the night. I thought I'd like to stay on the train for the whole week.

But the lady who was keeping an eye on me said she thought Hamden was the next stop. She was right. Because just then the guard came in and said, "This is your stop, young lady." I liked the way he called me *young lady*. He picked up my bag for me, too, and helped me open the heavy train door.

Hamden was a very small station and I was the only one getting off the train. The guard passed me my bag. I looked around. I suddenly thought, *What shall I do if Grandad isn't here? What if I'm stuck all alone in the middle of nowhere?*

But Grandad was there. An old man who looked a bit like a tramp came running down the platform. He had wild white hair and a wild white beard and he was shouting, "Molly! Molly!" The next minute he'd lifted me off my feet and was swinging me round and round.

Well! That was the first surprise. Dad was right. Grandad wasn't at all doddery. The second surprise wasn't so nice. Grandad didn't smell too good! I was glad when he put me down!

The third surprise was the tandem. Grandad had left it outside the station in the empty car park. The tandem was a rickety old thing with a big basket at the front. Grandad put my bag and One-eyed Ted in the basket.

"This is Lola," said Grandad. He gave the bike a pat as if it was a dog. "It's nearly as old as I am but still good for a bit longer."

Perhaps Grandad was a bit mad, I thought, to give his bike a name. Maybe being on his own so much was making Grandad go a bit funny.

"I think we need a little practice on Lola," said Grandad.

The tandem was quite tall. Grandad had to lift me onto the seat at the back. Then he got on at the front. We had a set of handlebars and pedals each. The tandem was like two bikes stuck together.

"The trick is to keep in time as you pedal," said Grandad as we set off. "Left pedal! Right pedal! Left pedal! Right pedal! That's it! You're getting it!"

We went round and round the car park about ten times. We were very wobbly at first but after a while I began to enjoy it. It reminded me of a dance Emma and I had done last term when we had to make sure we kicked up the same legs at the same time.

"Right," said Grandad when we'd gone round the car park one more time. "Now Lola can take us home."

Chapter 3
Cake and Ketchup

We wobbled, wibbled and shook our way to Grandad's cottage. The tandem didn't have any gears. There was a brake but I don't think it worked very well. Every time Grandad wanted to stop, he just shouted, "Whoa!" and put his feet on the ground.

We had to stop quite often. "To get more puff," Grandad said. When he'd got his puff up, Grandad sang.

Bumpety Bump, Bumpety Bump,
Here comes the Galloping Major!

After a while, I joined in. I joined in
because we were going down a dark, bumpy
track and singing made me feel a little less
scared. All I could see was trees. Trees and
shadows. Spooky shadows where anything
or anyone might hide. I gripped my
handlebars as hard as I could and made my
pedals keep going in time with Grandad's
pedals. Down, down, down the track we
bumped with everything in the front basket
shaking. One-eyed Ted's one eye peered out
at me. He looked rather surprised.

"Here we are!" said Grandad at last.
"Home sweet home."

This, I thought, really *is* the middle of
nowhere. There were no muddy fields – at
least none that I could see. Just trees.
Grandad's cottage seemed to be in the

middle of a wood. It made me think of Hansel and Gretel. And witches.

Grandad opened the cottage door. Out rushed two big dogs, one shiny black cat and a hen! Was this some kind of mini zoo?

"You shouldn't be here," said Grandad to the hen and shooed her out of the house. The hen stalked off as if Grandad had hurt her feelings.

"Meet Lop and Bop," said Grandad as the dogs jumped around us. They were wagging their tails and licking Grandad's face. "And this is Sweet Sue," said Grandad. He bent down to stroke the sleek black cat that was rubbing itself round his legs.

Inside the cottage everything looked as old as Grandad himself. And dusty! My mum's the dust-buster of all time. I thought she would call the police if she saw all the dust on Grandad's old dresser and on his piano and on the arms of his rocking chair.

We were in Grandad's kitchen. It was a kitchen and living room all in one. There was a squashy old sofa which Lop and Bop settled down on. Sweet Sue curled up in an old shopping basket.

"Here we are then," said Grandad. "Would you like something to eat?"

It seemed a long time since I'd eaten my sandwiches so I said, "Yes please, Grandad."

Grandad used the sleeve of his jacket to wipe some sticky stuff off the table. Then he fetched a cake from a cupboard and a bottle of tomato ketchup.

"Someone told me that children eat tomato ketchup with everything," said Grandad, "so I got this specially."

"That was very nice of you," I said. I was as polite as I could be. "But I don't think I'll have any with the cake."

Grandad looked disappointed. He made us both a mug of tea and we sat at the kitchen table eating the cake. We didn't know what to say to each other. Inside the cottage and up close, Grandad was even more stinky. Lop and Bop didn't mind. They came and sat under the table and caught the crumbs we dropped.

"What do we do next?" asked Grandad. We'd both eaten two slices of cake and Lop and Bop had gone back to the sofa.

I'd already seen that Grandad didn't have a telly. And as it was late and there didn't seem to be anything else to do in the middle of nowhere, I said, "Well, when it's as late as this Mum tells me to get washed and go to bed. And clean my teeth."

"Oh yes," said Grandad. "Washing and bedtime and teeth. I'd forgotten all that. It's a very long time since your father was a little boy. And then your grandma looked after him most of the time."

"I'm sorry about Grandma," I said.

Grandad looked sad. "She died many years ago but I still miss her."

"Mum and Dad say that you like living on your own."

"At first, after your grandma died, I didn't want to see anyone," said Grandad. "But I've got very lonely here now. I've been thinking ..." Grandad put his arm across the table and held my hand. "Would you like a new grandma?"

"A new grandma?"

"Yes," said Grandad. "I thought you could help me to catch one."

"Catch a grandma!" I said, astonished. *He's not just a little bit mad,* I thought. *He's very mad. I'm in the middle of nowhere with a mad grandad.*

"I've got a plan," Grandad said. "I'll tell you about it in the morning. I expect it's past your bedtime now, isn't it."

"Very," I said.

Grandad went up some dusty stairs and I followed him. My bedroom didn't look as grubby as the kitchen and there was a nice bright patchwork quilt on my bed. I took One-eyed Ted out of my bag and set him on the pillow.

"Your grandma made that quilt," said Grandad. "Each patch tells a story."

"Like the pages of a book," I said.

"Sort of," said Grandad. He pointed to one of the cotton patches that had a pattern of small blue flowers. "That's part of a dress your great-grandma wore when she was a girl. And this one here," he pointed at a yellow checked patch, "is from your father's pyjamas when he was five!"

Grandad seemed to have forgotten all about washing and teeth so I thought that just for once, I'd forget about them too.

I snuggled down under the patchwork quilt with One-eyed Ted snuggled next to me. The quilt felt somehow friendly with all those memories stitched into it.

When Grandad had gone downstairs I got out my mobile phone. I'd told Mum and Dad I'd text them to say I'd arrived safely. I thought I'd tell Mum about the dust too. She might be so upset she'd come and collect me at once. But I couldn't get a signal. My mobile wouldn't work.

"What d'you expect," I said to One-eyed Ted, "in the middle of nowhere."

Then I switched off my light and lay in the dark. I listened to the trees shushing and hushing. I heard Grandad creaking about downstairs. After a while something small and dark flopped on my bed and gave me a fright. But it was only Sweet Sue. She curled up by my feet and I was pleased to have her there.

It took me a long time to get to sleep. The trees seemed to be whispering secrets and I kept thinking of Grandad's plan to catch a new grandma. Was he going to kidnap one?

Mum and Dad will be very sorry when I'm locked up for kidnapping a granny, I thought. And then I fell asleep.

Chapter 4
Hens and Hope

When I woke up it was very, very quiet. Country quiet. Scary quiet. Middle of nowhere quiet. Sweet Sue had vanished. There was no sound of Lop and Bop and no sound of Grandad. Maybe he was off in the woods catching grandmas. I thought of my bedroom at home and all the friendly sounds I can hear in the morning – buses and cars and people talking in the street.

"Even the trees have stopped talking here," I said to One-eyed Ted. I held him tight and crept downstairs in my pyjamas. The kitchen was full of sunshine and empty of Grandad. The front door was wide open. I saw what I hadn't seen the night before. No muddy fields, but all the spaces between the trees full of green moss and bright leaves. And there was Grandad with a whole crowd of hens round him. There were at least six of them and they were all clucking and chucking like mad. Lop, Bop and Sweet Sue lay on the grass watching.

"Hello!" said Grandad. "The hens want their breakfast. Want to feed them?"

So I put my wellies on over my pyjamas and went out. The hens had lovely, golden brown feathers and sharp, bright eyes. They had a little house of their own. Grandad gave me a scoop of seed and I scattered it on the ground for them. It was nice having

them bustle about my feet, pecking and pecking. I remembered the lady on the train and how she'd said I might make new friends in the middle of nowhere. Maybe Lop, Bop, Sweet Sue and the hens could count as friends even if they didn't talk and talk and talk like Emma did.

"I suppose you want some breakfast too," said Grandad. "Like some more cake?"

"I don't think too much cake is good for me," I said. I was beginning to think that Grandad needed some help in learning how to look after children.

"Not good for you, eh?" said Grandad. He gave a grin that made me think of my dad saying, "Joke, joke". "Well, how about a fresh egg from the hens and some bread?"

So that's what we had. Lop and Bop went back under the table and Sweet Sue curled up in her basket.

"Now then," said Grandad, as he wiped some egg off his beard with a very grubby hankie, "about my plan."

"Oh, *that* plan," I said. I tried to make my voice as gloomy as I could. "The 'catch a grandma' plan. I don't think you'll find any grandmas around here."

"It's not just *any* grandma," said Grandad and his eyebrows shot up into his wild white hair. "I've got one in mind. I think I've fallen in love with her."

"In love?" I said. My eyebrows don't shoot up like Grandad's, but I felt as if they did. "At your age?"

As far as I know, people can only fall in love when they're young. Emma's sister, Peggy, is 16. Emma says she's always falling in love. Emma says that's because you need to practise falling in love and that Peggy has to practise because she's looking for the Right One.

"Why shouldn't I fall in love if I want to?" Grandad asked. He sounded huffy.

I didn't know how to answer that. I remembered once Mum had told me that when some people get very old they go into a second childhood. Maybe Grandad was heading that way. He was into his *second teenage.*

"Who is she then?" I asked.

Grandad got all excited. "Her name's Alice," he said, "and she works in the village shop ..."

"A shop? There's a village with a shop?" It was my turn to feel excited. A shop, any kind of shop, meant we were not quite in the middle of nowhere.

"Of course there's a village and a shop," said Grandad. "And my lovely Alice works there."

"Not *your* Alice yet," I said.

"No," said Grandad sadly. "That's the problem. That's where you come in."

"Me?"

"Yes," said Grandad. "Alice won't even smile at me. But she likes children. If you come to the shop with me then she might smile at both of us. And after that I can ask her to marry me and hey presto! You'll have a new grandma! Now, isn't that a good plan?"

I thought there was something missing in Grandad's plan. But I was very happy to go to the village shop with him and see the lovely Alice. With luck there might at least be a few postcards that I could buy and send to Mum, Dad and Emma. As long as there was a post box in the middle of nowhere, too.

"OK," I said. "When are we going?"

"How about now?" said Grandad.

Chapter 5

Smelly Onions and Bath Bubbles

The village shop was at least five miles away. Five miles uphill riding on Lola. We were both hot and puffed by the time we got there. I wondered if my face was as red as Grandad's, which was very red. And sweaty.

It was the sort of shop I like. It was small and sold all the sorts of things that everyone needs like bread and milk and vegetables and biscuits, but it had books, toys and postcards, too. And a shelf which said *Everything here under 20p*. The shop door opened with a nice little jingle and in we went. Grandad was as bouncy and hopeful as Lop and Bop had been when they thought they might get a few crumbs from our breakfast.

The lovely Alice was behind the counter. She was a small, plump woman, very neat and clean and with her hair curled up on her head like the ice cream in a cone.

"Good morning, Miss Alice," Grandad boomed. "I've brought my grand-daughter, Molly, to meet you."

"Good morning, Mr Martin," said the lovely Alice without even the flicker of a smile. Grandad's pong was even worse after

our bike ride. I think the lovely Alice was trying not to hold her nose.

But she gave me a big smile. "Has he made you ride that bone-rattler of his?" she asked me. And I was the one who got the smile.

"You can have something from the 20p shelf," she said. "A present because you're new here."

Grandad dug me in the ribs with his elbow. "Thank you," I said. "And I want to buy some postcards."

"You go and choose, dear," said the lovely Alice. She went on smiling at me.

I found a neat little notebook with an elastic band round it on the *Under 20p* shelf. I was just looking at the postcards when I heard Grandad get out his shopping list. And then I knew why Grandad's plan was going wrong.

"I'd like a loaf of bread, a bag of potatoes and lots of love and kisses," said Grandad.

"Really, Mr Martin," said the lovely Alice, "I don't think that's at all funny."

"It's not meant to be funny!" said Grandad.

But by then the lovely Alice had put the bread and potatoes in a bag. "Please don't speak to me like that again," she said.

I thought Grandad was going to cry. His old blue eyes looked very watery. He stood there, all scruffy and sad in his trousers with baggy knees and his shirt with egg on the front and his hair which looked as if it hadn't been combed for about six months.

And then I looked at the lovely Alice, all neat and clean behind the counter and I felt very sorry for Grandad being all lonely in the middle of nowhere.

So when I gave the lovely Alice the money for the postcards, I said, "My grandad's the best grandad in the world." It just came out like that without my thinking about it.

The lovely Alice looked rather surprised, but she just put the money in the till and said, "I'm sure you're right, dear."

"Come on, Grandad," I said. "Let's go home."

Grandad pedalled very slowly. He didn't sing 'Here Comes the Galloping Major'. Even Lola seemed to creak as if she was sad, too. I felt cross with the lovely Alice. Even if

Grandad *was* a bit smelly, how many people do you meet who ask for a loaf of bread, a bag of potatoes and lots of love and kisses? The lovely Alice didn't know how lucky she was!

And we didn't even need the potatoes! Grandad grew his own. He grew leeks too. And onions. And lettuces and carrots and sprouts. The potatoes were very heavy in the bike basket but by the time we got back to the cottage, I felt better. I had a plan of my own.

Lop and Bop came jumping and barking out to meet us and even the hens seemed to be chuckling.

"Grandad," I said, after Lop, Bop, Sweet Sue and the six hens had all had their tea and we were having ours, "your plan didn't really work, did it?"

"No," said Grandad sadly.

"Well, perhaps we can try mine," I said.

Grandad looked a bit more cheerful then. He gave me another bowl of soup. It was leek and potato which he'd made from his own vegetables and it was very good indeed.

"First of all, perhaps we need to tidy you up a bit," I said. "When did you last look at yourself in the mirror?"

"Let me see," said Grandad. "It might have been 1985!"

We went up to Grandad's bedroom and opened the wardrobe. There was a mirror inside the door. I wiped the dust away and Grandad looked at himself and said, "Oh dear! Oh dear, oh dear!"

It took us almost all of the next day to tidy up Grandad.

After we'd fed the hens, we pulled up the onions. I helped Grandad tie them together into long strings and we hung them up on the kitchen wall. The onions were golden brown, like the hens. I think we were both a bit smelly after that. So I asked Grandad if I could have a bath.

"A bath?" said Grandad as if he'd forgotten he had one.

"Yes," I said. "And if you had one too I could let you have some of my bath bubbles."

Grandad got quite excited at the thought of bath bubbles. When he had his bath I heard him splashing about in the bubbles singing,

Daisy, Daisy, give me your answer, do!
I'm half crazy, all for the love of you!
It won't be a stylish marriage,
I can't afford a carriage,
But you'll look sweet upon the seat
Of a bicycle made for two!

After Grandad had his bath I cut his hair for him. It still looked a bit wild, but it was clean now and not so long. And I cut his beard so you could see more of his face. And I dug about in the wardrobe and found lots of clean shirts and trousers. They were all very old, of course, but they were clean.

"Tomorrow," I said, "we'll go back and see the nasty Alice ..."

"The *lovely* Alice," said Grandad.

"All right, the lovely Alice. And you'll take her some flowers. Then you can invite her back for tea. And you won't say anything about love and kisses."

"I won't say anything about love and kisses," Grandad promised.

"And we'll both smile," I said.

"We'll both smile," said Grandad. "Do you think that will work?"

Chapter 6
Catching a Granny

Grandad told me some more stories about the patchwork quilt that night. There was a white silk patch with flowers stitched into it.

"That's from your mother's wedding dress," said Grandad.

Sweet Sue curled up on my bed again. As I fell asleep I thought about the lovely Alice.

Could she make patchwork quilts? I thought I might ask her.

In the morning we set off on Lola again. This time Grandad was looking very tidy and clean. He'd cut a bunch of buttercups and roses from his garden to give the lovely Alice.

The lovely Alice looked very surprised when Grandad gave her the flowers. They had gone a bit floppy by the time we got to the shop, but Alice put them in a jug at once.

Then Grandad gave a small bow and said, "Miss Alice, my grand-daughter Molly and I would be very happy if you would accept our invitation to tea. Please."

The lovely Alice looked Grandad up and down and sniffed once or twice. Then she blushed. She patted her ice-cream cone hair and said, "That would be very nice, Mr Martin. The shop is shut on Thursday afternoon. Shall I come then?"

And Grandad said, "That would be lovely, Miss Lovely. I mean Miss Alice."

Then they both giggled. *Second teenage,* I thought.

We had a lot to do before Thursday. I dusted the house. Grandad mopped the

floors. We even brushed Lop and Bop until their coats shone. Grandad made another cake like the one he'd made me. "I can only do chocolate cake," he said.

"Chocolate cake will be fine," I said.

And at three o'clock the lovely Miss Alice bumped down the bumpy track in a little blue Mini.

She took to Bop and Lop and Sweet Sue at once. And after a while, she rather took to Grandad. She took to the chocolate cake too!

While we were eating it, I asked her if she could make patchwork quilts.

"I'm not very good at sewing," she said, "but I can play the piano."

So Grandad lifted the lid of the piano. The lovely Miss Alice sat down and played 'Here Comes the Galloping Major' and Grandad sang and they both laughed over the bumpety bump bits.

I was sorry I was going home the next day because I was beginning to think the lovely Miss Alice might make a nice new grandma.

Grandad took me to the station in the morning and gave me a big hug.

"I think your plan might have worked!" he said. "I'll let you know."

****

"Well," said Mum, when I got home, "did Grandad look after you?"

"I think I looked after Grandad," I said.

Mum looked as if she didn't believe me.

But I knew I was right because about a year later we had a letter from Grandad. He said he was going to get married again and would we like to come to the wedding?

"What! A wedding in the middle of nowhere?" said Mum.

"No" I said. "A wedding in the middle of roses, buttercups and hens."

And it was.

Barrington Stoke would like to thank all its readers for commenting on the manuscript before publication and in particular:

Emily Barton
Ellie Buttrick
Maddison Carroll
Mitchell Cherry
Ben Clarkson
Joe Cooke
Ciara Corradi-Chirnian
Tom Cotter
Tegan Cutter
Luke Dean
Alice Doven
Teegan Gallagher
Molly Giddings
Aaron Harrison
Harriet Henshaw
Fiona Hislop
Florence Isaacs
Gabrielle Lyons

Ben Marks
Anthony Nardi
Jessica Newman
Rikhil Patel
Lauren Pattison
Catherine Pitt
Machaela Ridge
Sophie Ryan
Katelyn Salafia
Shannon Louise Simth
Martin Stevens
Alexander Stewart
Scott Troldahl
Sheridan Valenta
Emma Walsh
Dinah Wilcox

Become a Consultant!

Would you like to give us feedback on our titles before they are published? Contact us at the e-mail address below – we'd love to hear from you!

info@barringtonstoke.co.uk
www.barringtonstoke.co.uk

Also by the same author ...

The Crazy Collector
by Diana Hendry

Do you collect things? Stamps? Spiders? CDs? Tess has some really crazy collections. Or at least that is what her brother, James, thinks. But he can hardly believe his ears when Tess tells him what she plans to collect next!

You can order _The Crazy Collector_ directly from our website at www.barringtonstoke.co.uk

More exciting BRAND NEW titles!

Get That Ghost To Go Too! by Catherine MacPhail

Dean's back ... and this time he's angry!

Dean, the ghost, has made friends with Baggie Maggie, the local witch. That spells trouble. Now Maggie's plastic-bag magic has made Dean a real boy – and he's out to get Duncan and the gang. Can they get that ghost to go ... again?

You can order *Get that Ghost To Go Too!* directly from our website at www.barringtonstoke.co.uk